Genita

Thanks so much for your support

Get Up And Be Somebody! ™

God Bless

get up and
BE SOMEBODY

Copyright © 2009
by Lecia J. Rives
www.leciajrives.com

Cover design
by Anthony Waldren & Starvin Artist Graphic Design
www.starvinartist.net

If I Can Help Somebody lyrics
© Copyright 1944 by LaFleur Music Ltd.
Reprinted by permission

All rights reserved. No part of this book may be reproduced, copied, stored in a retrieval system, or transmitted in any form or by any means graphic, electronic, mechanical, including photocopying, recording, scanning or otherwise – without the prior written permission of Lecia J. Rives/ Speak uP! Enterprise Publishing, except where permitted by law.

ISBN: 978-0-615-21342-2

Printed in United States of America

For information:
Speak uP! Enterprise Publishing
P.O. Box 642
St. Louis, MO 63118

if i can HELP SOMEBODY...

If I can help somebody
As I pass along,
If I can cheer somebody
With a word or song,
If I can show somebody
He's trav'ling wrong,
Then my living shall not be in vain.

–Alma B. Androzzo

dedication

For three of my favorites:
My mother, Mable L. Rives
My father, Lenoir W. Rives
My dear cousin, JoAnna Jones

You are affectionately missed.

table of CONTENTS

ACKNOWLEDGEMENTS	7
PREFACE	10
TRUCK DRIVER	15
DOCTOR	17
RESTAURANTER	19
SONGWRITER	21
CLOWN	23
MECHANIC	25
MAIL CARRIER	27
DANCER	29
ARCHITECT	31
COMEDIAN	33
COACH	35
JUDGE	37
SUPERMODEL	39
MOM	41
CARTOONIST	43
VOLUNTEER	45
PILOT	47
BROTHER	49
FLORIST	51
PHILANTHROPIST	53
RECEPTIONIST	55
HOMEMAKER	57
SISTER	59
TEACHER	61
PHOTOGRAPHER	63
ARTIST	65

JANITOR	67
OPERATOR	69
DAUGHTER	71
FATHER	73
BARBER	75
CEO	77
GRANDMOTHER	79
TAXI DRIVER	81
PASTOR	83
FIRE FIGHTER	85
STRANGER	87
ENGINEER	89
INTERIOR DECORATOR	91
VETERINARIAN	93
METEOROLOGIST	95
CASHIER	97
BUS DRIVER	99
ATHLETE	101
FRIEND	103
TEENAGER	105
CARPENTER	107
DENTIST	109
CUSTOMER	111
PARAMEDIC	113
EPILOGUE	114
ABOUT THE AUTHOR	115

Acknowledgements

"We all have drunk from wells we did not dig and have been warmed by fires we did not build." -Anonymous

In an effort to complete this work, I am indebted to many for their care, support and expertise. Thank you, God, for providing me with ridiculous blessing and incredible peace. Without you, none of this would be possible.

Family

To my siblings, Mary, Dwight, Janet, Cedric and Eric, thanks for always looking out for me. Our parents would be proud of how you've taken care of their baby! To my godparents, Nino A. Fennoy and Toni Bellamy, for your unselfish love and continued guidance. To the Rives, Campbell, Smith, Dean, and Floyd clan, you're the best family ever.

Professional Team

Doris E. Massenburg, my twelfth grade creative writing teacher. Thank you for coming out of retirement to edit this book. Ever since I met you, you've pushed me to be a better writer. Thank you for preserving the integrity of my work and connecting with my passion. It was an absolute joy working with you. Let's do this again! Narmen Hunter, you are the best life coach on the planet! Thank you for helping me navigate this convoluted dream into a beautiful reality. Look what we've done! Jahmal T. Davis, Esq., thanks for all your efforts and legal savvy. I owe you. Anthony

Waldren, thank you for your patience and phenomenal creativity. Suzzane Skinner, thank you for taking a chance on me and my vision. Kim Wood Sandusky, you are wonderful!

Mentors

Laura Randolph Lancaster, thank you for taking me under your wing over twelve years ago and believing in my abilities. From passing the bar exam to writing articles to publishing this book, you've been an unparallel blessing in my life! Jackie Joyner-Kersee and Bobby Kersee, thank you for exposing me to another world and enabling me to fly. Cheryl Mayberry, thanks for always encouraging me to follow my dreams. Alexis Lewis, thanks for assisting me in getting to the next phase of my life. Pastor G. Vincent Dudley, Sr., and Glenda Dudley, your spiritual guidance and continuous prayers are a blessing. I am grateful for both of you and the entire New Life family. Amelda Jones, you are a jewel. Whatever you do, don't stop praying.

Friends

"True friends are like diamonds, precious but rare… ." – Unknown
Denitra Rives Seals, thanks for everything from kindergarten to college: "You and me us never part" (The Color Purple). Terease Baker Bell, thanks for your unyielding friendship. You're the best. Tiphany Rives, thanks for encouraging me to follow my dreams. Now go to your destiny. Kevin and Traci Roberts, you said I should, thought I could, and I did! Dackeyia Q. Sterling, thanks for all of your inspiration and prayers. Now it's time to cel-

ebrate. Regina Greer, thanks for always being there. Raquel Farmer-Hinton, thanks for your support and kindness. Hector and Tene Cummings, thanks for your contagious friendship. Felicia Keener, thanks for cheering for me and drowning out the naysayers! Ali Ryan Scott, thanks for always believing. Ale'Gryan Harris, thanks for your encouraging words. You were right! Lisa M. Butler, thanks for always caring. Albert Long, thanks for everything.

Supporters

To everyone who assisted me along the way in every aspect of my life, thank you!

preface

I recently visited my alma mater Tennessee State University to moderate a panel at the Student Leadership Conference. After the session, I had the honor of meeting the Student Government Association president, the fifth elected female to hold this position in the university's history. I was the second! During our brief conversation of southern pleasantries, I couldn't help noticing her remarkable resemblance to my younger self. She, like me, was so ambitious, so gifted, so determined, and yet so unaware of the complexities and uncertainties that assuredly awaited her at the altar of indecisiveness and future self-doubt!

Although I've enjoyed respectable success and endured substantial loss since my glorious collegiate days, I was surprisingly saddened to see the ME I used to be and apologetically ashamed of the ME I had become. The strong-minded ME, who once resolved that the apathy of existing is not worthy to be compared to the true art of living, had been shrouded behind a few fashionable quotes, an ever-increasing vernacular and a plethora of unimplemented ideas. The deliberate progressive ME, who once subscribed to the belief that the essence of service must be deeply imbedded in an articulate mission, moralistic values, and guided principles, had somehow shifted to arrogance and egoism.

In many ways I'd fallen into an abyss of mediocrity. It was difficult for me to acknowledge the authenticity of this painful truth because the visibility of my external accomplishments consistently overshadowed the invisibility of my internal struggle. Subconsciously, I had converted to a doctrine of "acceptable norms," which I often exploited as a substitute for excellence.

Then I remembered something. I remembered that somber autumn day I was mindlessly conducting my A.M. routine and I answered the phone to the reprimanding voice of my eldest sister--who, by the way, crowned herself family matriarch ten years ago--going on an early morning tirade about my niece, who, by all accounts, was trapped between life and living and too disconcerted to select one over the other.

Seventeen minutes into this excruciating lecture to which I committed only minimal attention, my sister, exasperated and spent, said something that would change my mind forever. She almost whispered, "All she needs to do is get up and be somebody."

Get up and be somebody.

Get up and be somebody?

GET UP AND BE SOMEBODY!

Those words enveloped me like an avalanche. For the next several days, then weeks, and eventually months, I pondered their message but remained inactive. I couldn't get the reverberation out of my head, as it aggressively chased me through the hallways of my imagination. And even though the statement sparked my thoughts with an unusual current of electricity, I was so unplugged from the passion of my core that my determination was paralyzed.

Invariably, my niece and I were one in the same.

Approximately, one thousand eight hundred and twenty-six mornings have passed since that disturbing epiphany, and I often think about the people who get up to be somebody and the overwhelming majority who haven't seized the opportunity to do so.

For most of us, life happens somewhere between bliss and disappointment, and our day to day routine often silences the fervor gnawing in the pit of our soul. Before long, years of life are washed away and our glossy daydreams are swapped for pale visions. Not to mention, the courage to become our best self has long been abandoned in search of an inexpensive replica.

Truth is, none of us know how much time we have left, and so the urgency to be the somebody we were created to be is critical. Perhaps you think your contribution is too small. Or maybe you even think that someone else can very easily do your part. Yet, what if your contribution isn't too small? What if it's so big that it could change the course of history or, even greater, the life of someone else?

Well, this is a book of inspirational and motivational snippets about ordinary people who make extraordinary impacts on the lives of others every day they decide to GET UP AND BE SOMEBODY!

Although only one percent of these stories happened either to me or to someone I know, the other 99% take place on the playground of my mental gymnastics; however, it is my sincere desire that 100% of these anecdotes will resonate in the inner depths of your heart and tickle the butterfly in your soul.

Get Up and pray

Truck Driver

Get up, Truck Driver! It's time to check the fuel levels and the oil.

The delivery you've been entrusted to make today is more important than you could ever imagine. There is an enthusiastic young scientist in Massachusetts waiting on the cargo you are assigned to transport. His research efforts are critical to the life of a little girl in Good Hope, Georgia, whom he has never met. He doesn't even know that she exists. Unbeknown to him, she's been waiting on a cure for an ailment with which she has suffered since birth. Today, the young scientist may create the formula tha makes her whole.

So, drive safely and back off the hammer. A little girl in Good Hope is depending on you.

Get Up and Care

Doctor
6:19 a.m.

Get up, Doctor! You have patients to see.

One of those patients is 79 year old Annie Ruth Johnson. Ms. Annie Ruth has had a long, hard, tedious life. She worked in a laundry facility from the time she was seventeen until she retired four years ago. The burn marks on her arms are painful reminders of an occupation she held for far too long.

Today, after surprising her 71 year old neighbor, who is less mobile than she, with her very first birthday cake, Ms. Annie Ruth will journey out the side door of her dilapidated home, take three buses to get to your office, one of which she will miss because the driver didn't notice her flagging him to wait, making her fifteen to twenty minutes late for her appointment. But when she proudly walks in on her cane, smiling with gratitude, you are quickly reminded of why you went to medical school in the first place, to help indigent people just like her. So today, it won't matter that she has temporarily misplaced her Medicaid card for the month because, unlike many of her previous visits, today will be different. The days of rushing patients in and out the door like widgets on a conveyer belt are over. Today, your beside manner will be impeccable and your attentiveness will be overwhelming. By most accounts this extra time spent may seem like a little thing to a lot of busy people, but this little thing will mean a great deal to an old woman who specializes in the care and concerns of others and yet she's been invisible to many for most of her life.

Get Up and Risk

Restaurateur

3:16 p.m.

Get up, Restaurateur! You have a pastry chef to hire.

Three years ago, Sarah quit her job as a waitress to chase her dream of becoming a pastry chef. For as long as she can remember, she has wanted to pursue a degree in culinary arts to express her love for making desserts, tarts, and other baked goods. She has sacrificed a great deal to invest in this dream, and in another year her dream will finally become a reality.

The question is not whether Sarah will make an excellent pastry chef. The question is whether or not you will leave your current occupation and open the restaurant you've been dreaming about so you can hire her!

Get Up and Write

Songwriter
4:31 a.m.

Get up, Songwriter! You have a song to write.

The musical composition and lyrics you dreamt about last night were not elusive. This poetic melody, like many others you've dreamt of before, has the power and ability to soothe a broken heart. The ballad that resides inside of you is full of rhythm, movement, color and contrast. It quite possibly could be one of the greatest songs ever written - if you'd just write it.

Remember the very first time you heard a piece of music that felt like bubble bath to your spirit. You know the kind of song that cradles you into the midnight when your ears are filled with tears. Well, this is that song for a nineteen year old in Coatesville, Pennsylvania, who will experience her first heartbreak within the next year. See, she won't immediately be able to discern that she'd be better off without him and that one day she'd barely remember his phone number. What she will remember, however, is the poignant lyrics that carried her through one of the most emotional periods in her life. As a matter of fact, she will never forget them. Every time she hears that song she'll do a little victory dance in her soul. And one day, when she's all grown up and has a daughter of her own, who will inevitably experience similar pain, she'll play that song for her.

Get Up and Celebrate

Clown

2:21 p.m.

Get up, Clown! You have a birthday party to attend.

I know you only started this job to earn extra money to purchase books for graduate school, but you're remarkable! Your antics and incredible energy have brought joy and laughter to hundreds of children. So, even though you plan to retire from this gig at the end of the semester, put on your best makeup, big red shoes, jovial attitude, and bag of tricks because today's party is special.

Today, Max is celebrating his sixth birthday. Ever since he was four years old, he has dreamed of having a clown at his party. He begged and pleaded with his parents to allow him to have one, and they promised to oblige him for his fifth birthday.

Well, his parents weren't able to make good on their promise last year because Max didn't spend his fifth birthday with them. Max was abducted shortly after his fourth birthday and returned to his parents only three months ago. So, the fact that you're entertaining at his party today is really a dream come true not only for Max but for his parents too.

Get Up and Conquer

Mechanic

9:13 a.m.

Get up, Mechanic! You have a car to fix.

The carburetor on that '92 Chevy has to be repaired today. I know you've been really busy and haven't had an opportunity to locate a suitable replacement for repair, but Theresa can't wait any longer. She needs to pick up her car today, and it is imperative that it's in perfect running condition.

Theresa will be traveling quite a distance to get to her mother's house in Magnolia, Arkansas, because today she summoned the courage to leave her abusive boyfriend.

Get Up and deliver

Mail Carrier
1:37 p.m.

Get up, Mail Carrier! You have letters to deliver.

Very few people tell you how much they appreciate you for the sacrifices you make to live out the mail carriers creed of "neither rain, sleet nor snow, the mail must go." But today a former law student will be extremely grateful that you didn't allow the rain to deter you.

In your mail bag, you have a very special letter from the National Bar Examiners in the state of Illinois. They just released the results from the July examination, and this particular letter holds the passing results for a young woman who took the exam seven times. She's been hoping and praying for this letter for the past seven years. So, even though she may not have an opportunity to thank you personally, she will be most appreciative that you, soaked but determined, delivered the answer to her prayers.

Get Up and dance

Dancer   5:04 p.m.

Get up, Dancer! It's time to dance.

Remember the last time you sashayed on the stage and started moving your physique with the effortless elegance a of swan. The wave of your arms from east to west and back again complimented the fluidity of movement from your mid torso all the way down to the strength in your toes. The dynamic equilibrium of your legs is a testament to your dexterity. You danced with a confidence that could be shattered by neither past fears or failures nor the tragedy of misfortune. Nothing could thwart the spirit of liberty that exuded from your being. You gyrated and twirled as if you were competing with the earth's axis, and you embraced a kind of freedom that only a few could even apprehend.

Well, tonight, James will be in the audience. He was released from prison two years ago for a crime he didn't commit, and, even though he's no longer physically incarcerated, he's still searching for the kind of freedom you've found. So, tonight when it's time to dance, dance like that!

Get Up and love

Architect

6:42 a.m.

Get up, Architect! You have skyscrapers to design.

The exterior design and magnitude of a skyscraper have always intrigued you. Even when you were a little kid, you often opted to draw tall buildings when all the other kids were coloring rainbows. And even though you enjoy your career immensely, you often question whether or not you're making a difference in the world.

Last weekend, Brittney and her father ate lunch in downtown Houston. On their walk back to the car, he informed her that he would be leaving for Iraq for the second time. As Brittney's little eyes overflowed with tears, her dad reminded her how much he loved her and promised her he'd return as soon as possible. Brittney, somewhat relieved by her father's reassurance, wiped her eyes, turned to her father, and said, "I love you, too, Daddy." When her father asked her how much she loved him, she pointed to the skyscraper across the street and said, "That much, Daddy!"

As her father fought back his tears, he took out his camera to take a picture of the building to serve as a visual reminder of his daughter's declaration. The skyscraper she pointed to was a building you designed ten years ago.

Get Up and Laugh

Comedian

8:19 p.m.

Get up, Comedian! You have jokes to tell.

You, unlike most people, have always loved your job. Even when you got started and used to get booed off the stage, you never considered doing anything else because you understood that the power of laughter could be a cathartic and an invigorating experience. As a matter of fact, you believed it was medicinal! Now you are so deliberate in your style and approach that somewhere between the intro and the punch line you've identified a launching pad that skyrockets your audiences into a stratosphere of amusement.

So, tonight when you see the hostess taking copious notes during your act, don't be alarmed; she's only hanging on to your every word so she can recite them to her mother tomorrow. Her mom is battling depression, and her prescribed medications are no longer effective. But when she hears your jokes, she laughs from the bottom of her soul to the top of her imagination. She often remarks that you're the best comedian she's NEVER heard!

Get Up and Motivate

Coach
2:38 p.m.

Get up, Coach! You have young people to encourage.

Many people wonder if you are going to retire since this is your thirty-fifth year. After winning numerous state titles, sending hundred of youngsters to college on athletic scholarships, and even witnessing a few of your former superstars enter into the pros, you finally ask yourself what more could there be? So, with all those accomplishments under your belt, you are strongly considering hanging up your whistle.

But before you make your final decision, ask that young man why he's sitting in the hallway on the floor with his ear affixed to the seam of the gym's double doors. His name is Charles, and he has been listening to you motivate your team while doing his homework for the past four years.

You don't know that Charles considers you one of his biggest supporters. Because of you, he is a graduating senior who will be attending college in the fall. See, Charles never knew either of his parents, and he and his sibling were separated in the foster care system when he was twelve. So, every time you shouted words of encouragement to the team, he pretended that you were talking to him.

Get Up and fight

Judge
10:08 a.m.

Get up, Judge! You have a courtroom appearance to make.

Immediately after you were sworn in, you quickly discovered that the best part about your job would also be the worst part about it. Back when you were conducting marriages, the euphoria you experienced uniting two lives was exhilarating. Now, since you've been transferred to divorce court, the melancholy of witnessing a family dividing simply breaks your heart. And sometimes it's staggering to know that the fate of the couple appearing before you has been intentionally placed in the rapping of the gavel in your hand.

Today, you'll be presiding over the divorce of the Carmichaels. Tracy and Jake Carmichael were high school sweethearts and have been married for nine years. Even though neither of them really wants to split-up, today is the last hearing before their divorce becomes final. Although you've been communicating with their respective attorneys for months, today you'll have an opportunity to speak to them face to face.

When they separately enter the courtroom and make a beeline to their designated seats, they stare at you with a curious intensity. Within moments they both realize that you are the same judge who married them nine years ago and separately begin to reflect on happier times.

Call it fate or call it a resurrection of faith, seeing you today gives them one more reason to consider calling a marriage counselor instead of calling it quits.

Get Up and Aspire

Supermodel

12:17 p.m.

Get up, Supermodel! You have a runway to walk.

Fashion shows, photo shoots, and magazine covers have been an integral part of your life since you were seventeen years old. From the beginning, your whole world has been consumed with various aspects of beauty - dazzling jewelry, resplendent clothing, glamorous places and radiant faces. Not to mention, you are the recipient of alluring compliments on a daily basis.

At today's fashion show, one of your biggest admirers will be watching you stroll up and down the runway. Cassy, a comely thirteen year old, has aspirations of becoming a model some day. But last year she was involved in a freak accident that stripped her of mobility in both her legs. In recent months she's undergone multiple surgeries and a plethora of physical therapy sessions. For a long time, she desired to look like you, act like you, dress like you, and talk like you. Ever since the accident, all she wants to do is walk like you.

So, today when you walk, you will do more than awe the fashion community, you will also fuel Cassy's determination to walk as well.

Get Up and Nurture

Mom
11:51 a.m.

Get up, Mom! You have daughters to nurture.

Children are one of God's most precious creations. As a mother, your children are on your lap when they're small and on your heart when they're grown. Because of this closeness you never really relinquish the maternal instinct to protect them from all hurt, harm, and danger, and the amount of energy you expend for them is unfathomable. That's why, when your oldest daughter gets pregnant with her first child, you rush out to buy her chunky monkey ice cream at her every request.

Today during your ice cream excursion, you will notice a young woman, who appears to be about eight months pregnant, struggling with her grocery shopping. The mother in you will instantaneously rise up and scurry over to help her. While assisting her with her shopping, the two of you will chat for roughly an hour. Near the end of your conversation, she won't be able to resist telling you that her mother died when she was twenty-six years old, and, when she found out that she was pregnant, it pained her heart to know that her mother could never assist her on days like today nor assuage her nervousness in caring for a newborn. When the two of you embrace to say goodbye, she will thank you for standing in her mother's stead today.

Get Up and Read

Cartoonist

2:17 a.m.

Get up, Cartoonist! You have sketches to create.

There is nothing quite like eating a bowl of cereal, watching the Saturday morning cartoon line up, and reading the comic section of the newspaper, especially the comics you create. Your comic strips are not only humorous but also relevant, bursting with expressive thought and life applications. The simplicity of your drawings coupled with the humanistic and ethical values infused in your characters is ingenious and commendable.

I'll bet you didn't know that every Saturday morning for the past few years Alex has been reading the cartoon strip to his father A.J., who is functionally literate and terrified to read aloud. Last Saturday's comic strip discussed the benefits of developing confidence; this Saturday, when it is time for Alex and A.J. to commence their Saturday morning ritual, A.J. will put down his bowl of cereal, pick up his newly developed confidence, and start reading the comic strip to his son.

Get Up and try

Volunteer

Get up, Volunteer! You have a heart to warm.

The reason you initially started visiting the nursing home was to impress your female classmates and earn extra credit in your sociology class. You weren't at all interested in doing anything other than passing the class to get your parents off your back and securing a few dates.

This afternoon when you get to the home, you'll meet Ed, an eighty year old angry, bitter man who appears to dislike everything and everybody. As a matter of fact, he's been bitter for so long that you will quickly discover why almost everyone avoids him and why the nurses call him mean and surly.

There used to be a time when Ed was a very jolly, likeable soul whose only dislike at the nursing home was perhaps the food. However, as time passed and his only frequent visitor, his niece, went away to college, he progressively started to despise everything in his surroundings.

Today, forget what you may hear about Ed and strike up a conversation with him. Later when you invite him to play a game of checkers, he won't be able to mask the sheer delight in his eyes. Contrary to popular belief, Ed is still a very warm and kind-hearted soul. He just needs you to show up today to remind him of what that looks like.

Pilot
5:26 a.m.

Get up, Pilot! You have a plane to fly.

International flight PK 712 to Pakistan is where you'll be headed. Although you never really cared much for flying internationally, this particular flight appears on your route and you reluctantly settle into the idea of flying abroad.

Today, before you board the plane to check the engines, controls, and instruments, you will overhear a conversation between a husband and his wife. The two of them will be absolutely elated about flying to Pakistan today because someone very special will be waiting for them when they land. When they arrive in Islamabad, they will unite with their adopted son Manuel. The adoption process in Pakistan was not an easy one, but, after several miscarriages and one still birth, the couple will receive the miracle for which they have prayed. Manuel will be the couple's first child, and they simply can't wait to welcome him into their lives and their home.

So, today when you're flying on automatic pilot, don't think about the length of the flight. Instead, reflect on how wonderful you felt the day your adoptive parents welcomed you into their home.

Get Up and lead

Brother
6:04 p.m.

Get up, Brother! You have a younger sibling to guide.

When you were ten years old, every third Friday of the month your Dad would bring home a model car for the two of you to put together. This was a very special bond shared exclusively by the two of you for nearly three years. On those occasions, your mind was like a sponge, and you absorbed every teachable moment your father and you shared. The man you are today was greatly inspired by the discourse that transpired between the two of you on those select Friday nights.

Unlike you, your younger brother was only three when your father was killed in the line of duty, and you knew then, as you know now, that your brother would never have the privilege of sharing the same type of bond with your dad as you did.

So, today, the third Friday of the month, go out and purchase a model car for your brother and you to put together. He's ten years old now and could benefit from those teachable moments. Not to mention, your dad is counting on you!

Get Up and believe

Florist
5:05 a.m.

Get up, Florist! You have flowers to send.

Although flowers have been a part of your world for as long as you can remember, you never imagined one day taking over the family floral business. After your parents retired a few years ago, you were the candidate to continue the forty year legacy because of your eye for color and aesthetics for flower arranging. Now your days and nights are filled with the selection of seasonal flowers, the reconciling of invoices, and the accounting of payroll taxes. So, every Monday morning when you turn on the shop lights, you are convinced that this isn't what they meant when they said, "Wake up and smell the roses."

However, this Monday morning when the fragrance of freshness wafts though the air, instead of daydreaming about some place better, you will be reminded of the weekly floral bouquet drawing scheduled to be implemented this week. And for today's recipient you couldn't have picked a better time to start. Barbara, this week's winner, will discover that her company is downsizing and her entire department is being eliminated. But, soon after she receives this news, she will receive the beautiful arrangement of sun-bursting yellow roses sent from your shop. She will inhale the sweet smell of a new beginning. And somewhere between the shock of losing her job and the surprise of receiving the lavish bouquet, she will exhale and realize that everything really is going to be all right.

Philanthropist
7:35 p.m.

Get up Philanthropist! You have a charity to spread.

You never really considered yourself a philanthropist because you've only given away small sums of money. However, philanthropy is more than the amount of money you're able to give; it's your benevolence toward mankind.

So, today when you're in the dollar store, focus more on the gift of giving as opposed to the amount of the gift. That way, when you approach the register to pay for the thirty items in your cart, you won't be apprehensive about asking the gentleman behind you if you can pay for his items as well. When you do this, you'll discover that philanthropy is contagious; the essence of a philanthropic gift is really the electricity in giving. The same gentleman whose items you just paid for will take the three dollars that he planned to use for his own purchase and hand them to the woman standing behind him. The two of you won't be aware that this woman will be calculating in her mind which three items she plans to return to the shelves due to insufficient funds.

So, even though you don't really consider yourself a philanthropist, the woman in the back of the line does.

Get Up and Encourage

Receptionist

Get up, Receptionist! You have phones to answer.

Suffice it to say, there is never a dull moment at your office. As a matter of fact, your middle name is multitasking, especially since a number of the employees in your department mistake your position for that of a secretary or an administrative assistant. From filing, to faxing, typing memos, sending emails, scheduling meetings, making calls, and answering the phone, you seldom have time to finish your morning coffee before noon.

Even though you've grown accustomed to handling a variety of tasks, the most essential function of your job is answering the phone. Therefore, having a pleasant phone voice is paramount. It's been said that people can detect whether you're smiling, frustrated, or having an awesome or awful day just by the inflections in your voice. A vibrant, cheerful tone can uplift a downtrodden spirit.

So, today when you're answering the phone, be exceptionally kind to the caller who dialed the wrong number. She's a runaway teen living on the streets. Today she finally musters the courage to call her parents, and your warm, friendly, soothing voice will be enough encouragement for her to hang up the phone and dial the number again.

Get Up and Envision

Homemaker

9:12 a.m.

Get up, Homemaker! You have cookies to bake.

Baking is your favorite pastime, and your homemade chocolate chip cookies with macadamia nuts have rock star status wherever they are served. The ingredients you use to whip up a batch of these delicious treats are incomplete until you sprinkle an ounce of love and pinch of compassion in the mixing bowl. When it's time for baking, the sweet aroma encourages feelings of contentment and comfort. If you close your eyes and inhale all at the same time, you can almost see the cute little house with the white picket fence.

So, today even though temperatures outside are below freezing and the winter mix of snow and sleet doesn't necessarily encourage a baking mood, bake up a few dozen batches of your round delights. Remember not to skimp on "the sprinkle and the pinch!" When you're all done, take them over to the homeless shelter across town. This may appear to be an insignificant gesture to you, but the homeless will appreciate the vision of a cute little house with a white picket fence.

Sister
5:21 p.m.

Get up, Sister! You have an older sister to mimic.

After twenty-one years, you are surprised to discover that you have an older half sister. Even though your mother and other siblings aren't accepting of your new found relationship, family is family to you. You learned to embrace the art of forgiveness a few years ago after losing your twin sister in a campus shooting. For months your anger and bitterness toward the perpetrator consumed you, stifling your productivity and derailing your relationships. Eventually, you realized that the domino effect of the pain held your ability to forgive hostage. So, after a period of healing you befriended forgiveness along with your older half sister.

So, this evening when the two of you go out for dinner and she informs you that she has been diagnosed with lupus, pretend that the two of you are kids and start playing the mimic game. If she cries, you cry. If she laughs, you laugh. Whatever her action, make that your reaction. After all, that's what little sisters do.

Get Up and teach

Teacher
8:02 a.m.

Get up, Teacher! You have students to teach.

You've been teaching elementary school for twenty-three years now; yet every fall when school starts you still get overjoyed when you see the toothless smiles of your new second grade class. As you write out the name cards of a few of the newcomers, like Rachel, Jarret, Thomas, Elizabeth, Yeheli, Anyi, Delarosa, and Natasha, you are eager to enhance their skills in mathematics, spelling and cursive writing.

Although "teacher" is the given title for your profession, for many of your students you have been so much more: like the time you bought socks for Riley to wear to the sock hop because she didn't own a pair without a hole in them; or the day you made cupcakes for Armani to give to the class because you knew his father wouldn't show up.

So, today after recess when Elizabeth asks if you think she can be an astronaut, look her straight in the eyes and tell her with conviction that she can be whatever she wants to be. This will be a defining moment for her because the last time she asked someone that same question that person told her she'd never amount to anything.

Get Up and Observe

Photographer

Get up, Photographer! You have a moment to capture.

It's been said that a picture is worth a thousand words. You knew the first time you heard the shutter of a camera lens that you wanted to be a professional photographer, but, ever since you had that disagreement with your parents, you can't seem to capture a breathtaking photo in a single frame to submit for publication.

So, today when you're out canvassing the city in search of an awe-inspiring shot, pause to examine the two elderly deaf men playing chess in the park. They will be engaged in a heated sign language debate over the last chess move. After you've observed a few exchanges, one of the gentlemen will sign to the other, "You're right. I'm sorry." In that flash of a moment a snapshot of beauty will unfold on the opposite end of your camera lens, and you will be reminded of how simple and picturesque an apology can be.

When you develop the prints, you appropriately entitle the series "Expressions of an Apology." After admiring the display, you submit the photographs for publication so that the stubborn, the unyielding will blink, soften, recognize, admit. Then you call your parents to express an apology of your own.

Get Up and Inspire

Artist 3:38 p.m.

Get up, Artist! You have a portrait to paint.

Every time you lack inspiration you think about your best friend, the former Miss Wyoming. Last year, she miraculously escaped death in a blast that disfigured her face and burned eighty percent of her body. When you look at a picture of how she used to look, you are saddened for her. But every time you speak with her, you are inspired by her effervescent spirit.

So, today in her honor, pull out your pallet and brushes, and paint her an incredibly beautiful portrait. Even though the painting won't resemble her present exterior, it will mirror her indomitable character and her majestic zest.

Get Up and aim

Janitor
7:58 p.m.

Get up, Janitor! You have waste baskets to empty.

When you envisioned yourself working in corporate America, being a janitor was not a part of that vision. You always imagined that you would be a team player in a big company, but somewhere along the lines that dream was derailed and you settled on the track of just securing a job. Your plan was to work in your current capacity for about a year or two and then go to college or trade school and do something more with your life, but it never seemed to be a good time to make a transition. In the meantime, you started treating emptying waste baskets as if you were the vice-president of a department as opposed to being trapped in some mindless occupation; that way you could practice for the job you wanted and focus less on the job you had.

So, today when you're emptying waste baskets on the thirty-third floor, pay special attention to the trash can in Sue's office. Sue accidentally knocked her thumb drive off her desk and into the trash while gathering up a number of documents. This particular thumb drive has a very important presentation on it that would take her weeks to recreate and cost the company significant dollars if the project is delayed. Exercise your VP mentality and place the thumb drive back on Sue's desk. This will be a substantial step toward becoming a team player in a big company.

Get Up and think

Operator 5:16 p.m.

Get up, Operator! You have a caller to comfort.

Everyday you get calls from kids playing on the phone, but today, when three year old Enrico calls to talk to you, he won't be playing. Listen to him, and, when you listen long enough, he'll tell you that his poppy is lying on the floor and his mommy isn't home. It will be important for you to continue to hold the line with him because it's dark in the house and he's afraid of the dark. But if you ask him to sing, he'll sing at the top of his lungs most of the words to "Jesus Loves Me" over and over again until the ambulance arrives.

Get Up and dare

Daughter
11:30 a.m.

Get up, Daughter! You have compassion to demonstrate.

Growing up you despised being the only child. When you were younger, you never understood why your mom did not have any other children, and you didn't find out until you were fifteen that you were a miracle baby. The doctors told your mom that she wouldn't be able to have a child, but five years later you came along. Your mom was so happy to have a little bundle of joy, and for decades your every wish was her command.

Six months ago, your mom had a massive stroke. After that everything changed and you had to care for her in ways you never imagined. Sometimes, it's overwhelming to keep up with the various medications you have to administer, and other times you wonder what more you could do to make her latter days better.

Today, when you're conducting your daughterly duties, Maria will be watching. Actually, Maria has been watching you for weeks, and she is absolutely swept away by the care and sensitivity you exhibit toward your mom. Because of your actions, today she will visit her own mother whom she hasn't seen or spoken to in over twelve years.

Get Up and Cheer

Father

Get up, Father! You have a son to support.

As a single parent working two jobs to raise a teenage son, you have--it's fair to say-- your share of challenges. But you made yourself two promises a long time ago: (1) your son would never want for anything and (2) you'd do everything you could to be the father for him that you never had.

Rumor has it that your son is a fledgling superstar in track and field, but you wouldn't know because you haven't been to a track meet. Although he's never invited you to come and support him, he's posted the schedule on the refrigerator every track season for the past two years.

So, today instead of going to your second job to keep your first promise, go and see your son run. It's not too late to keep your second promise and be the father for him that you never had.

Barber
6:24 a.m.

Get up, Barber! You have heads to shave.

It must be something about the swivel of your chairs and the humming of your clippers that gives your shop a palace appeal. For most men, the barber shop is a place to relax, confide, confer, create and manipulate reality, and occasionally even get a hair cut. For others, it's an oasis where million dollar memories are born and hundred dollar bets are lost. It's a passport to manhood for young cohorts and a platform of philosophy for an older generation. In fact, on any given day, it's a king's castle.

However, on Saturday mornings from 7:00 to 9:00 the "For Ladies Only" sign hangs in the window, making the shop a safe haven for women who have suffered significant hair loss from chemotherapy to get a clean head shave.

So, this weekend when Linda arrives with her hat pulled below her eyebrows and her face pressed against the glass to sneak a peak inside, she won't be embarrassed. This time, she can comfortably enter the front door of the king's castle and be among queens.

Get Up and Succeed

CEO

7:08 a.m.

Get up, CEO! You have some mentoring to do.

It took a long time for you to climb your way to the top. Long before you were a fixture on mahogany row, brokering deals in China, you were a lowly intern with lofty ambition. The first time you entered the right side of the revolving doors of a major corporation you wanted to exit on the other side. However, a gentleman named Mr. Osaki rescued you as you stood paralyzed in front of the elevator doors afraid to push the up button. He straightened your tie, gave you a word of advice, and took you under his wing for the next several years.

So, today when you see a flush-faced young man in the restroom with his tie peeking out of his pants pocket, he's not making a new fashion statement. No one ever taught him how to tie a tie, and he's too embarrassed to ask anyone on the first day of his new internship.

Lest you forget, today would be a good day to start repaying your debt to Mr. Osaki.

Get Up and trust

Grandmother

Get up, Granny! You have another child to love.

When your grandson Justin turned seven, he started bringing things home for you to nurture. First, he showed up with the turtle he found in the back yard. Next, it was the frog he stuck in his front pocket, unfortunately breaking all the frog's limbs. Last month it was the hamster that was really a mouse, but Justin didn't realize that.

In great part you are responsible for his save-the-world attitude. Early on, you taught him to love all living things, telling him that every single one of God's creatures deserves loving care.

So, today when Justin shows up with Solomon, a little boy whose parents are addicted to drugs, Justin will expect you to nurture and care for Solomon the same way you nurtured and cared for him when his mother struggled with addiction.

Get Up and Move

Taxi Driver

10:53 p.m.

Get up, Taxi Driver! You have a passenger waiting for you.

Driving cab # 756 is a drama even on a slow night. The checkered backgrounds of your passengers range from high to low class and sometimes no class at all. And once the meter starts running, you know that you're in for an evening of backseat confessions, manipulative lies and deception, and sheer unadulterated comedy. Having driven a cab for a while, you've learned the difference between good company, great people, and an excellent tipper.

Tonight, when you're passing by The Thunder Cat Bar and you see Steve staggering down the sidewalk en route to the parking lot with his keys dangling from his pocket, give him a ride home. He is too inebriated to be either good company or an excellent tipper. Yet tonight, if you choose, you have an opportunity to be a great person and do for Steve what you wished someone had done for your friend Malik the night he had been drinking and wrapped his car around a poll one block away from his house.

Get Up and Worship

Pastor
10:31 a.m.

Get up, Pastor! You have a sermon to preach.

It's been said that the church is like a hospital full of hurting people in search of healing. So, every Sunday morning when you stand in the pulpit to preach to congregants and visitors about hope, faith, charity, and repentance, you cannot overemphasize the importance of having faith.

So, this Sunday when you're giving your text and you identify Pastor Reynolds in the audience among the other congregants, resist the protocol to invite him to join you in the pulpit. Today he's just another patron desperately in search of healing, holding on to faith that he will find it in this Sunday's sermon.

Get Up and Imagine

Firefighter

Get up, Firefighter! You have a fire to douse.

When the alarm goes off at the firehouse in the middle of the night, you don't have the luxury of deciding whether or not you will answer the call. Like clockwork, you spring into action to save an endangered life. Sometimes it may be a cat high up in a treetop; other times it may be a frightened teenager trapped in a three story building, afraid to jump to safety.

Today, when you arrive at the three alarm fire, no one's life will be in jeopardy. The entire family will be safe, but the father will be in tears, not because the house he built with his own hands is burning to the ground right before his very eyes, but because he couldn't find the family photo album before he escaped the flames to safety.

So, when he asks to borrow your cell phone, he won't be trying to make a call. He just wants to take a picture of his family to remind him he has everything he needs to build and start again.

Get Up and Work

Stranger

Get up, Stranger! You have an acquaintance to make.

You've been on your feet all day working tirelessly in the world of retail. From the time the department store doors opened, it's been "Hey, miss!" and "Excuse me, ma'am!" bombarding you from every conceivable direction.

Dealing with the public is an art form all its own, but interacting with them during the holiday season brings about a completely different set of challenges, especially for someone who's already worked eight hours at another job.

Your sixteen hour day at an end, you walk briskly to your car. You notice an aged woman on the parking lot desperately searching for car keys. Even though your feet are screaming for relief, you stop to offer assistance. After scouring the immediate surroundings for nearly half an hour, you encourage her to abort her search and insist on giving her a ride home. She reluctantly agrees, and during the twenty-five minute drive she's constantly rummaging through her purse. When the two of you arrive at her estate and she exits your vehicle, she politely thanks you for your outstanding customer service, and, as a sign of her gratitude, she hands you an envelope. At home you discover in the envelope a thousand dollar check bearing a very prominent name. Instantly, it is apparent to you that the aged woman you just met was no ordinary stranger; she, along with her family, owns the retail chain for which you work.

Get Up and dream

Engineer

11:02 a.m.

Get up, Mechanical Engineer! You have a roller coaster to design.

You can't remember a time when you weren't fascinated by the physics of a thrilling roller coaster ride. The dynamics of the cars suspended seemingly in mid-air fueled your resolve throughout your tenure in the school of engineering. Even though you were one of only a few females in your class, you didn't allow anything or anyone to curb your enthusiasm for amusement parks and riveting coaster rides.

Today, several engineers will conduct a test run of the new apparatus you designed for riders who are slightly smaller than the normal height requirement stipulated for coasters of this magnitude. If everything goes as planned, the vertically challenged at Believe Academy will be extremely excited the next time they visit the Magnificent Kingdom Theme Park. Even though many of them are beyond their pre-teen years, some of them have never had the opportunity to experience the thrill of a roller coaster ride due to the various height restrictions.

So, today when you board "The Zinger" for your inaugural ride, let the sunshine dance on your face as you whisk through the triple loop. Today is a celebration for little people everywhere who once desired to ride a monstrous roller coaster but couldn't because they were too small.

So, hold on tight, and enjoy the moment. You've waited a lifetime for this opportunity, and today, despite your forty-one inch stature, you're as tall as your dreams.

Get Up and Create

Interior Decorator

11:06 p.m.

Get up, Interior Decorator! You have a space to create.

Fabrics and paintings and furnishings, oh my! Your creation of ambiance via hues and textiles to effect mood and movement is your signature touch. The energy you invest in aesthetics is commendable. Although you have a fixation with shades and tints, it's minute compared to the sensation you feel when coloration and feng shui embrace.

You have your Aunt Lucy to thank for your obsession with impression. When you were just a little girl, she taught you that atmosphere was everything. So, today when you're decorating the guest room where she will be staying, make it vividly and tactilely charming. Although Aunt Lucy's blind now and she won't be able to appreciate the aesthetic charm of the room, she won't be able to deny the tingling sensation solidified by woven textile patterns, cashmere, cotton and silk.

Get Up and Sing

Veterinarian

Get up, Veterinarian! You have a swallow to assist.

Your love for animals supersedes your love for almost anything else. Your special care of your patients is essential since they cannot articulate their ailments, and every encounter of an injured or afflicted animal pricks your heart.

Some of the most gratifying moments of your life are connected with your profession: performing a successful surgery on the family cat, watching a Shih Tzu recover in rehab, or delivering a colt. Nothing, however, gives you greater pleasure than helping a needy stray.

So, this evening when you observe outside your office window a little lame bird that appears to be suffering from a simple fracture, please help. This fine feathered creature chirps a concerto outside little Katy Madison's bedroom window.

For the past four months Katy has been wetting her bed, but every morning when she hears the melodious sounds of birds paying homage to the daybreak, she sluggishly awakes from her dreamy slumber and gets out of bed to go potty.

Get Up and Soar

Meteorologist

Get up, Meteorologist! You have a forecast to announce.

Being on television has always intrigued you, and, when you landed the job at KIRO as a meteorologist, you couldn't have been more excited. The nifty slogans printed on umbrellas and rain hats alike became synonymous with your name and made you an instant local celebrity in a quaint rainy city.

Although you only utilize your knowledge of atmospheric science to predict the weather, try convincing your four year old nephew Javier that the wind and the rain are beyond the span of your control.

Javier is an expressive little wonder who only deviates from his daily cartoon marathon twice a year to view your weather forecast. Each time he tunes in is in anticipation of his grandpa's biannual visit. On those occasions, Javier obsessively monitors the weather to determine whether or not the conditions will be permissible for the three of you to drive up to Seattle to fly kites on Kite Hill.

Flying kites is a new fascination for Javier, who was born with no hands, and he enjoys kiting with his grandpa, who recently lost both his legs. Together, they are an awesome unbeatable pair, and nothing, short of turbulent winds coupled with upper Northwest drizzle, can rain on their parade. So, follow the weather patterns closely, for Javier will be watching.

Get Up and push

Cashier
12:23 p.m.

Get up, Cashier! You have an order to correct.

The fast food industry is so predictable. Despite the availability of a multitude of choices, repeat customers seldom deviate from their usual orders regardless of how often they visit the drive-thru.

You're so good that you've memorized the ordering patterns of many of your frequent customers, and, once you recognize their voice, you can remember the make and model of their vehicle before they arrive at the window.

The driver of the pearl Cadillac Escalade always requests that you hold the mustard. The guy who drives the navy Ford Escort doesn't particularly like tomatoes, and the lady who drives the silver five-speed Honda Accord always orders her sandwich on wheat without the cheese, not because she doesn't like cheese, but because cheese doesn't like her.

So, today when the lady in the silver five-speed Honda Accord orders her sandwich without any special instructions, don't ignore your instinct to ask her if she wants you put that on wheat and hold the cheese. Today, she's succumbing to the pressure of caring for her elderly cousin who's suffering from dementia, and she just needs a little push to remember the simple ways to care for herself.

Get Up and prove

Bus Driver

Get up, Bus Driver! You have some stops to make.

All kind of riders utilize public transportation. Some ride due to a lack of private transportation, while others ride to avoid the woes prevalent in a big city, but all ride en route to another destination.

It is a well known fact in the city that you have one of the best routes on the bus line, not because of the cleanliness of your bus, but because of your entertaining comments and optimism. As each rider exits, you remind him or her that there is a miracle on every corner.

Alice has been riding on your route to and from auditions for the past year. After each long exhausting day of rejections, she eagerly anticipates hearing your motivational tidbits and sage advice.

So, today when Alice boards the bus at the corner of 6th and Daniel rejoicing because she finally landed a small part in a big play, it's because you played a big part in a small way.

Get Up and build

Athlete
11:49 a.m.

Get up, Athlete! You have a dream to fulfill.

After all the years of hard work and dedication, it felt like the top spot of the Olympic podium was built just for you. You remember the very first time you watched the Olympics. It was a sweltering day in the summer of 1960 when you sat on the living room floor of the family's four room non-air conditioned home. Seated Indian style, you cradled your chin in the palm of your hands and affixed your eyes to the old black and white television set with an antenna made out of a wire clothes hanger laced with aluminum foil. You sat in astonishment as members of the USA team raced to victory, and from that day forward you aspired to become an Olympian.

You've come a long way since your humble beginnings, but every time you visit your crime-ridden, poverty-stricken hometown you're reminded of how far you have to go. So, today when Amber doesn't ask for your autograph but for a safe place to play instead, you realize that you have to build a special place for kids just like her so that anywhere they stand they too can experience the exhilarating feeling of standing on the top spot of the Olympic podium.

Get Up and Shine

Friend

1:07 a.m.

Get up, Friend! You have a hand to hold.

You didn't see Brenda for twenty-five years after she had been whisked off to Greensboro, North Carolina, at the end seventh grade. You remember how sad you were that she wouldn't be able to participate in math club with you anymore, especially since she was the smartest person on the whole team.

Even though Brenda had a reputation of being the smelliest girl in the entire school and most kids called her "Stinky Skunk" rather than Brenda Monk, you always called her "Best Friend." She solidified her title the day you failed to solve the easiest math problem during the 9th Annual Classic Math Bowl Competition and the team lost the championship by one point to the cross town rivalry. Instead of avoiding you like the plague like all your other teammates, Brenda sat beside you on the bus and held your hand as the tears silently fell from your eyes like raindrops on a cotton ball.

So, today when the two of you embrace for the first time since middle school and she thanks you for being her friend, she really means it. She always wanted to confide in you about her hygiene, and today she'll tell you that her stepfather molested her from the time she was eight until she moved to Greensboro. Back then, she thought if she smelled he'd leave her alone. Ultimately, her plan to salvage her innocence failed her, but your friendship never did.

Get Up and Continue

Teenager — 4:04 p.m.

Get up, Teenager! You have loud music to play.

The only thing better than securing your driver's license at age seventeen is blasting hip hop music while joy riding with friends in your parent's sleek SUV. However, on this particular occasion you leave the house without your arsenal of rap music, and the only compact disc in the vehicle is Gloria Gaynor's 1979 rendition of "I Will Survive." Your inability to ride in silence persuades you to push play, and after the third repeat you decide to commit the lyrics to memory and begin to sing along.

When you approach the stoplight, you fail to notice the police car pulling up beside you. As the officer moves his hand towards the switch to flash the lights and blare the siren, he is paralyzed by the music emanating from your sound system. Instantly, he recognizes the song and reflects on his youth.

His sister used to play this song all the time after their parents were killed in a car crash. Over the years this song has served as an anchor of survival for him through two divorces, type II diabetes and recovery from a mild heart attack.

So, today instead of pulling you over for disturbing the peace, he rolled down his window, smiled and sang along.

Get Up and Execute

Carpenter

3:14 a.m.

Get up, Carpenter! You have a freeway overpath to measure.

Over the years you've honed your skills from apprentice to master carpenter. Your carpentry math is so precise that you're highly sought after for numerous projects throughout the state. After a while, all the projects run together.

However, today when you're working on highway 40, don't think of it as just another project. It's important that you produce your best work and insist on higher barriers for motorist protection. A few years from now Tommy will attempt to commit suicide by careening around the semi sharp curve, flipping his pick-up truck over the side railing. If he succeeds, his car will plummet onto Jessica, who is driving along a different path en route to Chicago to pursue her dream of becoming a clinical psychiatrist.

Get Up and Smile

Dentist
1:09 p.m.

Get up, Dentist! You have teeth to clean.

Dentistry is your ministry, and, when you volunteer to clean teeth at the local clinic, kids who may not receive a cleaning otherwise are able to experience the mint taste of their tongue running across a smooth set of pearly whites.

So, today when Mandy asks you for twenty-eight extra toothbrushes to give to her classmates for show and tell, please supply her with them. She is so excited about her clean teeth that she wants to share it with the whole class. Even though there are only twenty-seven kids in her class, she's saving the twenty-eighth one for her great grandpa; although he already has a tooth brush, Mandy thinks the teeth in the water glass beside his bed may need one too.

Get Up and Serve

Customer

11:59 a.m.

Get up, Customer! You have a waiter to tip.

Since you've been retired, having lunch with your goddaughter has become a monthly tradition. The two of you chat and chew at the local Red Lobster about all sorts of things. At the conclusion of the main course, you always grab the bill and insist on paying. Customarily, you use this as an opportunity to unload at least fifty extra dimes you've either found or collected over the course of the month.

So, today when you calculate the tip for the waiter, be sure to leave the usual extra. When the server tears up at the additional amount, it's because this is one of three jobs he maintains to pay for his college tuition and every dime counts.

Get Up and be

Paramedic 12:00 midnight

Get up, Paramedic! You have lives to save.

Every time the operator dispatches the 911 call your heart pounds like a bass drum leading the percussion section in a marching band. The intensity you feel as you approach the scene of the intended patient is unsettling.

Even though you've lived in the neighborhood all your life, you seldom have any acquaintance with the human life lying prostrate on the gurney. Yet, the spiritual connectivity is overwhelming. Perhaps it's because you've had a near flat line experience and felt the devastation of a dream expiring. This kind of anxiety fuels the idea that death is the grand theft of untapped greatness; dying with talents unexpressed is tragic. Contrary to the saying that "you can't take it with you," unused talent you really can take with you! Taking "it" with you usually signifies that you never share "it" with anyone else.

So, today when you arrive at the address of destiny, do whatever you can to save The Dreamer who carries the dream. Pull out the shock paddles to revive The Visionary before the vision dissipates. There's a world in waiting, anticipating the gift that has been embedded in each of us. It's the gift that everybody has to get up and be somebody.

epilogue

For years I've lived in neglect. I've neglected my gifts and talents, neglected my dreams, and inevitably neglected some strangers along the way who've been waiting for me to enhance their lives in one way or another. I have assumed that time was on my side regardless of how many wakes and funerals I've attended. I thoughtlessly believed that when I was ready I could shift gears and make life happen through me instead of allowing it to happen to me. Then one day I realized that time is a great enemy too. So I pleaded with God not to allow me to die with my gifts and talents hidden within me.

Oftentimes we are dismissive about our gifts and talents. We convince ourselves that unless we find a cure for cancer or make an indelible mark in a third world country we cannot significantly impact the world. I submit, however, to every reader of this book that the things we do everyday on our jobs, in our homes, and within or outside our community greatly impact someone else's tomorrow. This book is meant to be a reminder of the simpler things. I hope after reading these pages you make a commitment from this day forward to be and do! This is the beginning of the rest of your life. Cherish every moment. Take advantage of every breath. Don't allow someone else to suffer as a result of your disobedience. Today is all you have, and, if you do what you have been carefully selected to do, today will be all you need. So, take courage and get up and be somebody. Someone, somewhere is waiting for you. Time is ticking. Can't you hear it?

About the Author

Lecia J. Rives is the president of Speak uP! Enterprise. This East St. Louis, Illinois, native is a graduate of Tennessee State University and Howard University School of Law and the executive director of the Jackie Joyner-Kersee Foundation. She is also an adjunct instructor of public speaking at Washington University in St. Louis, Missouri, a contributing writer for *In Magazine*, a comedienne and an attorney who does motivational speaking and workshops around the country.

Pledge

I, _____, from this moment forward, pledge to Get Up And Be Somebody. I will not allow fear, excuses, past failures, or disappointments to deter me. I refuse to live a life of untapped greatness. Today I will take my place in the sun!

_____
Name

_____
Date